Text copyright © Jeremy Strong 1997
Illustrations copyright © David Mostyn 1997

First published in Great Britain in 1997
by Macdonald Young Books
an imprint of Wayland Publishers Ltd
61 Western Road
Hove
East Sussex
BN3 1JD

Find Macdonald Young Books on the internet at http://www.wayland.co.uk

The right of Jeremy Strong to be identified as the author of this Work and
the right of David Mostyn to be identified as the illustrator of this Work
has been asserted by them in accordance with the Copyright, Designs and
Patents Act 1988.

Designed and Typeset by Backup Creative Services, Dorset DT10 1DB
Printed and bound in Belgium by Proost International Book Production

British Library Cataloguing in Publication Data available

ISBN 0 7500 2359 7

JEREMY STRONG

Aliens in School!

Illustrated by David Mostyn

MACDONALD YOUNG BOOKS

Chapter One

Max came home from school one Christmas
almost bouncing with excitement. He
couldn't wait to tell his mum and dad the
news. Max always looked excited, even
when he wasn't. This was because he had
wild, shaggy hair that stuck up from his
head like a box of exploding straws. He
wore big fat spectacles that made his eyes go
bulgy. In fact he looked rather like a crazy
inventor.

This wasn't surprising, because Max's dad really *was* a crazy inventor, and Max looked just like him, except that Dad also had a big bushy moustache that wiggled about under his nose like a large and friendly caterpillar.

As soon as Max reached home he went racing out to the shed where Dad did all his inventing. "Guess what, Dad! There's going to be a Christmas party and everyone's going in fancy dress and there'll be prizes and loads of food and everything! What shall I go as? What shall I wear?"

But Dad didn't seem to hear him. He was far too excited himself. He pushed his son into the shed. "You're going to like this, Max," he said. It was dark inside and Dad groped around, crashing into things and tripping over before he found the coil of knobbly wire he was looking for. He draped the wire round Max's chest and strapped a small box to his head. "Now, jump up and down," said Dad.

Max jumped, and tiny fairy lights along the wire began to light up. In fact every time Max made any movement at all the coloured lights flickered into life. "The energy you make by jumping up and down lights up the bulbs," explained Dad. "This is my latest invention – The Walking Christmas Tree. If there's a power cut on Christmas Day people can put lights on themselves instead. Tell me I'm very clever."

"You're very clever, Dad," said Max. "As you're so clever, why don't you invent me something to wear for the fancy dress party?"

"Too busy," said Dad cheerfully. "I've just had an idea about goldfish. Ask your mother."

Max's mum was in the middle of drum practice. Bish-bash, bishy-bash! she went, trying to twirl her drumsticks and getting one stuck up her nose. "Bother! I did it really well just now, when nobody was looking."

"Mum, what shall I be for the fancy dress party at school?" asked Max.

"I know just the thing – Father Christmas."

"Father Christmas! Mum – that is *so boring*! There must be something better – *please*!"

Mum shook her head. "What could be better than going to a Christmas party as Father Christmas? We've got an old costume your father wore years ago. I'll hunt it out for you."

Max groaned. Father Christmas! This was going to be the worst Christmas party ever. His friends would die laughing.

Chapter Two

Far out in deep space a small alien craft
was rapidly approaching Planet Earth,
whizzing along at hyperlight-speed.

*Who were these strange aliens? What were
they up to?*

They were Gobbs, from the Planet Gobble – and Planet Gobble, despite its name, was a planet that did not have a single crumb of food of its own. Because of this, the Gobbs had to hunt the galaxies day and night for any food they could find with their jellyscopes. (A jellyscope is similar to a telescope, but it picks up signs of food rather than stars.)

Slobb Gobb was the boss of this alien gang. Like all Gobbs he had a big mouth, and a fat green tongue like a piece of old carpet covered in mould. His lizard-like skin was covered in purple blotches.

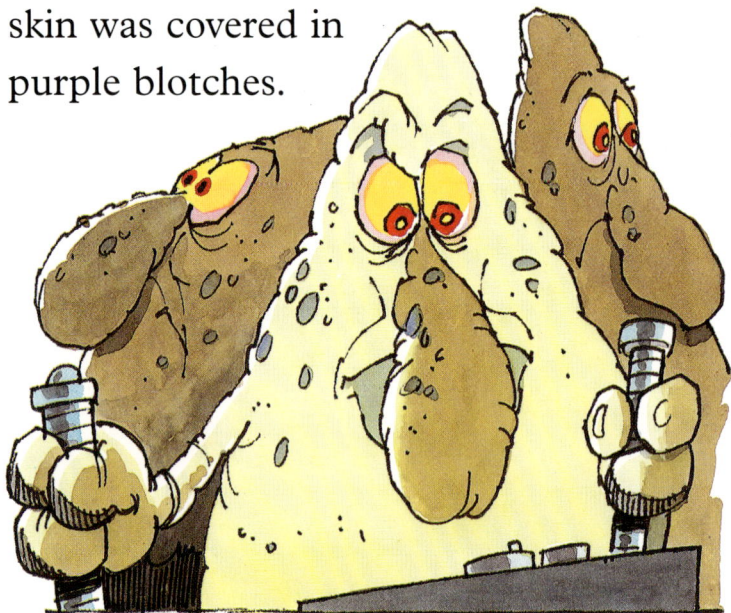

Yobb Gobb and Blobb Gobb were the crew, and to tell you the truth all three Gobbs looked exactly like each other. You'd have to be a Gobb yourself to tell them apart. So, if you *can* spot any differences between them… well, you know what that means!

The Gobbs were hunting for food. Blobb Gobb had been searching deepest space with his powerful jellyscope, pointing at every planet to see if he could spot any grub. The Gobbs were quite happy to scoff just about anything, but jelly was top of their interplanetary shopping list.

Fixing the jellyscope on Planet Earth, Blobb gave a loud, triumphant blurp.

(Humans slurp and humans burp, but Gobbs blurp.)

"I spy jelly, a jelly jamboree, a jolloppy jelly – two different colours!"

"What colours? What colours?" blurped Slobb Gobb.

"There's red jelly!" cried Blobb.

"Wohwohwohwoh! Red jelly! Red jelly in my belly!" Slobb began dancing round and round the spacecraft.

"And… *there's green jelly*!" whispered Blobb in awe. There was a dull thud as Slobb Gobb crashed to the floor and began furiously waving his little legs in the air.

"Green jelly! Wohwohwohwoh!" The Gobbs hardly ever found green jelly. Green jelly was like caviare for a Gobb.

"Have you got a fix on the jelly-source?" demanded Yobb. Blobb peered down the jellyscope and nodded.

"Bagbush Primary School, Britain. Steer six-nine-one, speed five thousand millispex. We'll be arriving tomorrow afternoon. Aren't they going to get a nasty shock!"

"Aren't they just!" muttered Yobb, and a hungry froth appeared round his big smackery lips. "We'll have their jelly or we'll splat them all over with our Splatter-Blatters!"

"Yeah!" blurped Blobb. "Planet Earth – here we come!"

Chapter Three

That same evening, Max stared gloomily out of his bedroom window. In the morning he'd have to dress up as Father Christmas and everyone would laugh at him. The shame of it!

It was dark outside, but Dad was standing in the goldfish pond. He was covered in twinkling Christmas fairy lights. "Good, isn't it?" Dad called out.

"This time I'm using goldfish energy to create enough electricity to power these fairy lights."

"But why, Dad?"

"Well, Max, if you get tired of jumping up and down on Christmas Day..."

"... you can go outside and stand in the goldfish pond," Max finished for him. "Somehow I don't think many people will be interested, Dad."

"No? Oh well, never mind," Dad said happily, and he carried on stirring the goldfish pond with a little stick that had a plastic shark tied to the end.

Max shut his window and was about to draw the curtains, when –

Ting!

Max had an idea. Why not go to the fancy dress party as The Walking Christmas Tree? Nobody else would be going as a Walking Christmas Tree, all lit up. He'd wanted Dad to invent him something all along. It was an excellent idea. Max threw open the window again. "Hey, Dad? Can I borrow The Walking…"

At that moment there was a loud
KER-BOOM!! Dad shot from the pond
in an explosion of water and landed high
in the apple tree.

"Are you all right?" shouted Max
anxiously.

"Yes, I'm fine – just a bit surprised. I'm afraid I've blown up all my fairy lights."

Max groaned. That put an end to The Walking Christmas Tree costume. "There's a goldfish stuck behind your ear, Dad," he muttered, and went to bed in a bad mood.

Things did not improve the next morning when Mum gave him the Father Christmas costume. "You'll look lovely, Max," she said.

"I'll look totally stupid," grumbled Max, stuffing the costume into a big plastic bag. He wasn't going to let *anyone* see what an idiot he looked until the very last minute.

When Max reached school he almost gave up in despair. The other children looked really good. There were witches and pirates, spacemen and a whole kingdom of princesses.

"What are you going to be, Max?" his friends kept asking.

"Embarrassed," Max muttered under his breath.

"Ooooh!" they cried. "Mopey Max is in a mood!"

Off they went to watch all the food going into the hall for the party. There were sausage rolls, cheese on sticks, mountains of sandwiches, and chocolate biscuits galore – not to mention great wobbly bowls of jelly. (Red and green!)

At last the children were allowed into the hall. What a sight! The tables were shiny and decorated and loaded with food.

Max could not put off changing into his costume any longer. He stomped off to the cloakroom and pulled on the Father Christmas outfit, stuffing a pillow inside to make himself fatter. The beard felt horrible and prickly, and Max reckoned he must look a prize twit.

Max was heading for the hall when a flash of light from the playground caught his eye. He glanced out of the window and his boggly eyes gave their biggest boggle ever.

An alien spaceship was hovering right over the netball court!

Max watched it land. He saw the door
open and a ramp come down with a hiss
and a clang. And he saw all three Gobbs
wave their Splatter-Blatters and go
marching into the school. Max turned
deathly white.

Aliens! Aliens were invading!

Chapter Four

Into the school went the Gobbs – one, two, three – chanting as they marched. "Red jelly! Green jelly! Red jelly! Green jelly!" They stamped up the corridor and reached the doors to the hall. Slobb Gobb pointed his Splatter-Blatter.

"Stand by for attack!" he blurped.

Splammm!!!!

Max was hiding at the end of the corridor, quaking in his Father Christmas boots. This was awful! He *must* get help. He crept off to the school office, picked up the telephone and dialled 999.

"Police? This is Bagbush School. Aliens have landed in our playground and they're attacking us."

"Oh yes, sonny? And my name's Donald Duck."

"No really! Please! You've got to help!" pleaded Max, but it was no use.

"Now listen to me, sonny boy, stop wasting my time or I'll tell your headmaster."

The phone went dead. Max almost cried. This was a nightmare. No! It was far worse than any nightmare. At least you woke up from nightmares, but this was for real!

Max crept back towards the hall and peered through the doorway. The Gobbs were standing on the stage. The headmaster, Mr Duff, seemed to think that he was talking to three children in fancy dress.

"Splendid costumes!" cried Mr Duff cheerfully. "You *do* look convincing. I award you First Prize in the fancy dress competition and I'd like to present you with these book tokens." Mr Duff handed three envelopes to the scowling aliens. "Now, who's hiding under those masks? I bet it's the Grabbly brothers! Let's have a look!"

Slobb Gobb aimed his Splatter-Blatter at the headmaster's face, then reached up and pulled Mr Duff's beard, rather hard. "Stupid hairychin!" he snarled.

"I beg your pardon," cried Mr Duff. "That's not very polite."

"Stop gabbling!" blurped Slobb. He turned his Splatter-Blatter on the school piano and – **Splammm!!!** – there was no piano, just a giant mountain of dribbling glue. Mrs Rump, the music teacher, fainted.

"Give us all your jelly!" roared Slobb. "We want the jelly – *now*!"

"And the cheesy things!" added Blobb.

"Yeah, the cheesy things *and* the choccy-bix!"

"If anyone moves, we'll gloopify the lot of you!" threatened Slobb. "Now, it's jelly time! Let's get jellified! Wohwohwohwoh!"

Slobb Gobb threw himself from the stage and landed with a loud *splurp!* on the jelly, where he instantly began blurping and generally making a mess of himself and everything around him.

The children and teachers huddled together in a terrified silence as they watched the Gobbs start gobbling up their Christmas party food.

Max gazed from the doorway in desperation. What was he to do?

Chapter Five

The Gobbs were very busy, face down in the jelly, but nobody in the hall dared move a muscle. They were frozen by fear.

Max realized that he was the only person in the school that the Gobbs didn't know about. If only he could surprise them and give the teachers a chance to overpower them... What Max needed was a weapon for himself.

He scanned the corridor. He spotted a mop, but somehow he didn't think the Gobbs would be scared by a mop, even if it was still damp. Then he saw a big fire-extinguisher. That was better. At least it *looked* threatening.

Max lifted the extinguisher from the wall. It was so heavy he almost dropped it. He grasped it tightly and poked the nozzle out in front of him. Then he took a deep breath – and he let it out again. This was truly scary.

The Gobbs went plunging across the tables, scattering food in every direction and yelling like babies. They scampered out of the hall, down the corridor and into their spaceship. The ramp hissed into place. The door shut with a clang and a moment later the Gobbs went whizzing away into space. It was all over in seconds.

Nobody was more surprised than Max. He was so astonished he dropped the fire extinguisher.

Shhlliiiissssshhhh!!!!

The extinguisher jolted into action and foam sprayed everywhere. The more Max tried to stop it, the more he spread it about. Half the school got extinguished.

"Whoops!" murmured Max.

The headmaster staggered across the hall, splattered in foam. "Father Christmas!" he cried. "You've saved us!"

"It's me!" said Max, pulling off his prickly beard. "What happened? What did I do?"

"Max! Well done!" said Mr Duff. "Those aliens thought you were some terrifying creature – a Fat Red Monsterthing. Anyhow, they've gone! We can have our party after all."

And that is exactly what they did. There
was still plenty of food left – even jelly –
and everyone went home full to bursting.
Max wandered back with some of his
friends.

"I don't think those Gobbs should have
got First Prize for the fancy dress,"
complained Samantha.

"No? Who do you think should have won?" Max asked.

"Haven't got a clue." Samantha looked at him and giggled. "It wouldn't be Father Christmas, anyhow. You look really silly."

"I'm not Father Christmas," said Max coolly. "I'm The Fat Red Monster-thing, and I've just saved the world, so there!"

Look out for more titles in the Red Storybooks series:

Dinosaur Robbers by Jeremy Strong

Tyrannosaurus and Triceratops may look real, but they're actually two robotic dinosaurs invented by Max's dad. However, Buster and Binbag's beady eyes spy the dinosaurs and decide they'll come in handy for a spot of burglary...

Magic Sponge by Michael Coleman

Is Barry Biggs ever going to get on the school football team? It's not much fun always standing on the touchline with Mr Simkin's bucket of water and sponges. But then Barry discovers Captain Tripp's *magic* sponge and thinks his big chance to be a star has come at last...

Thomas and the Tinners by Jill Paton Walsh

Thomas works in the tin mine where he meets some fairy miners who cause him a great deal of trouble – but then bring him good fortune. WINNER OF THE SMARTIES PRIZE.

The Disastrous Dog by Penelope Lively

When the Ropers bring a dog home from the animal sanctuary, they have no idea what they have let themselves in for. Soon the dog has the whole family running in circles round him.

You can buy all these books from your local bookseller, or they can be ordered direct from the publisher. For more information about Storybooks, write to: *The Sales Department, Macdonald Young Books, 61 Western Road, Hove, East Sussex BN3 1JD*